The HAUNTED LIBRARY

FOR THE REAL
MR. HARTSHORN

THANK YOU FOR READING A SHY SIXTH-GRADER'S "NOVEL" ALL THOSE YEARS AGO AND MAKING HER BELIEVE SHE REALLY COULD BE AN AUTHOR WHEN SHE GREW UP—DHB

* * * * * * * * * * * * * * * * * *

No author ever publishes a book all alone. I'd like to thank my agent, Sara Crowe, and everyone at Grosset & Dunlap for their support and all their hard work on my behalf.

* * * * * * * * * * * * * * * * * *

GROSSET & DUNLAP
Published by the Penguin Group
Penguin Group (USA) LLC, 375 Hudson Street, New York, New York 10014, USA

USA | Canada | UK | Ireland | Australia | New Zealand | India | South Africa | China

penguin.com
A Penguin Random House Company

Text copyright © 2014 by Dori Hillestad Butler. Illustrations copyright © 2014 by Aurore Damant. All rights reserved. Published by Grosset & Dunlap, a division of Penguin Young Readers Group, 345 Hudson Street, New York, New York 10014. GROSSET & DUNLAP is a trademark of Penguin Group (USA) LLC.
Printed in the USA.

Library of Congress Cataloging-in-Publication Data is available.

ISBN 978-0-448-46246-2 (pbk)   10 9 8 7 6 5 4 3 2 1
ISBN 978-0-448-46247-9 (hc)   10 9 8 7 6 5 4 3 2 1

The HAUNTED LIBRARY
The GHOST BACKSTAGE

BY DORI HILLESTAD BUTLER
ILLUSTRATED BY AURORE DAMANT
GROSSET & DUNLAP ✱ AN IMPRINT OF PENGUIN GROUP (USA) LLC

GHOSTLY GLOSSARY

EXPAND
....
When ghosts make themselves larger

GLOW
....
What ghosts do so humans can see them

HAUNT
....
Where ghosts live

PASS THROUGH
....
**When ghosts travel through walls,
doors, and other solid objects**

SHRINK
....
When ghosts make themselves smaller

SKIZZY
....
When ghosts feel sick to their stomachs

SOLIDS
....
**What ghosts call humans, animals,
and objects they can't see through**

SPEW
....
What comes out when ghosts throw up

SWIM
....
When ghosts move freely through the air

WAIL
....
What ghosts do so humans can hear them

CHAPTER 1

GHOST SKILLS

*C*uckoo! . . . *Cuckoo!* . . . *Cuckoo!* . . . *Cuckoo!* . . .

"Kaz!" Beckett said sharply. "Are you listening?"

Kaz *was* listening. But he was listening to the cuckoo clock chiming in the library entryway. He was not listening to Beckett.

"What's the matter, boy?" Beckett asked as he floated around the craft room. "Why are you so distracted?"

Kaz bit his bottom lip. "Claire's late," he said.

Claire was a solid. She lived in an apartment above the library with her family. She could see ghosts like Kaz and Beckett when they weren't glowing. And she could hear them when they weren't wailing. No one knew why.

More important, Claire was Kaz's

friend. Kaz and Claire hadn't been able to spend much time together lately because Claire had started school last week. She didn't get home until three twenty in the afternoon. Sometimes even three thirty. But now it was four o'clock. Claire had never been *this* late before.

"What if something bad happened to her?" Kaz said.

"I'm sure she's fine," Beckett said. "You should be happy she's late. That gives you more time to practice your ghost skills."

Kaz groaned. Beckett had started working with Kaz on his ghost skills while Claire was at school. He said Kaz's skills were an embarrassment to all ghosts.

"No groaning!" Beckett barked. "Let's get back to work. It takes a lot of

concentration to pick up a solid object. You have to send all your energy to your hands as you reach for the object. Watch!" Beckett stared hard at the wall of books.

Kaz watched as Beckett *sloooowly* pulled a red book from the shelf.

"You can't think about anything other than picking up the object," Beckett said, his eyes still fixed on the book in his hands. "If you let your mind wander, the object will fall."

The book slipped through Beckett's hands and hit the floor with a loud thud.

Kaz's ghost dog, Cosmo, yelped in surprise.

"Now try to pick up that book," Beckett told Kaz.

Kaz wanted to learn to pick up solid objects. If he could master that one skill,

it would be so much easier to play cards or board games with Claire, because then he'd be able to hold his own cards and move his own game pieces.

Arms outstretched, Kaz kicked his feet and dove for the book. "Aaaah!" he screamed as his hands passed through it.

"Don't scream!" Beckett ordered. "Concentrate!"

Kaz stared hard at the book, like he'd seen Beckett do. He clenched his teeth . . . and reached for the book.

His hand passed through again.

"You're not concentrating," Beckett said.

"I am, too," Kaz said as he gave his hand a shake. He hated the feel of solid objects passing through his body. "It's just hard."

And Beckett wasn't a very patient

teacher. Not like Kaz's mom or pops. Or his grandparents. Or even his big brother, Finn.

Kaz sighed. He missed his family. He hadn't seen them in so long. Not since the old schoolhouse, where they all used to live, was torn down and all the ghosts inside had blown their separate ways.

"Try again," Beckett said.

Kaz was tired. He didn't want to try again. But he tried one more time, anyway.

Pick it up . . . pick it up . . . pick it up, he told his hands. He couldn't possibly concentrate any harder than he was already concentrating.

It was no use. His hands passed right through the book.

"Aha!" came a voice from the doorway. "I thought I'd find you here."

Kaz whirled around. "Claire!" he cried with relief. "You're home!" Maybe now he could take a break from his ghost skills.

Claire set her bag on the table in the middle of the room and skipped over to Kaz and Beckett. Kaz loved the sound of Claire's feet on the floor.

"Sorry I'm late," Claire said as she bent down to pet Cosmo. Her hand passed through Kaz's ghost dog.

Cosmo wagged his tail and licked Claire. Claire's cat, Thor, watched from the doorway. He didn't look happy about Claire giving Cosmo attention.

Claire didn't notice her cat's expression. "Guess what?" she said to Kaz and Beckett. "My school is putting on a play. They're doing *Jack and the Beanstalk*. And guess what else?"

11

Claire was almost bursting inside herself. "I got a part!" she squealed, jumping all around. "I get to play the mom."

"That's great," Kaz said. He liked plays. He and his brothers used to put on plays for their parents and grandparents back at the old schoolhouse. "Congratulations!"

"Thanks." Claire beamed.

Beckett grunted.

"What are you guys doing?" Claire asked.

"I'm trying to teach Kaz how to pick up a solid object," Beckett said. "But I give up. He's not concentrating. And now that you're home, he's even less likely to concentrate." Beckett stepped through the wall of books and disappeared into his secret room.

Kaz had never seen Beckett's secret room because . . . well, he wouldn't say he *couldn't* pass through walls. But he really, really didn't like to.

"I *was* concentrating!" Kaz called after Beckett.

"Don't worry about him," Claire said as she picked up the book and returned it to the shelf. "You'll learn how to pick up a solid object someday. I know you will."

Kaz wasn't so sure.

"I've got something else to tell you," Claire said, with a funny twinkle in her eye.

"What?" Kaz asked.

Claire leaned toward Kaz. "I think there's a ghost at my school."

"Really?" Kaz's heart leaped. "Is it someone from my family?"

Kaz and Claire had started a detective agency because Claire wanted to solve mysteries and Kaz wanted to find his family. So far they'd only found Cosmo. And that had been a lucky accident. They ran into him while trying to figure

out who was haunting Mrs. Beesley's attic.

Claire unzipped her bag. "I don't know," she said as she pulled out one of her notebooks. She had several of them. One was for keeping track of clues when they solved mysteries. Another was for keeping track of all the ghosts she'd seen. Kaz was pretty sure this one was the ghost book.

"I didn't see the ghost," Claire said as she opened her notebook. "This boy, Jonathan, saw it. He's in the play, too. He plays Jack!"

"What did he see?" Kaz asked.

Claire read aloud from her notebook: "Tuesday, October tenth. Budd Elementary School. Jonathan Bixby, fourth-grader, claims to have seen a ghost float through the stage curtain and fly around our school cafetorium."

Jonathan

Tuesday, October 10.
Budd Elementary School.
Jonathan Bixby,
4th Grader
claims to have seen a ghost
float through the stage
curtain and fly around
our school cafetorium.

"Ghosts don't fly," Kaz said. "We swim."

Claire wrote that down.

"What else did Jonathan say?" Kaz asked.

"That was all." Claire showed Kaz her notebook. "I didn't actually talk to him myself. He left right after tryouts. Probably because no one believed him."

No one ever believed solids when

they said they saw a ghost. Kaz didn't understand why.

"I think we should investigate," Claire said. "You should come to school with me tomorrow and see if you can find the ghost."

"What? Really?" Kaz asked. He'd never thought about going to school with Claire.

"Sure. Why not?" Claire said. "I can put you in my water bottle, like we did when we investigated Mrs. Beesley's haunted attic. What do you say?"

"I say, 'yes!'" Kaz exclaimed. Going to school with Claire would mean:

(1) A day off from his lessons with Beckett

(2) Extra time with Claire

(3) Maybe finding his family!

Kaz could hardly wait until tomorrow!

CHAPTER 2

OFF TO SCHOOL

N o," Beckett said the next morning while he and Kaz drifted around Claire's bedroom. Claire was in the bathroom, brushing her teeth. "You can't go traipsing off to school with that solid girl when you have your own lessons to work on right here."

"My lessons are coming along fine," Kaz said.

"Are they?" Beckett raised an eyebrow. "Can you glow? Can you wail?

Can you pass through a solid object or even hold one in your hand? These skills don't develop by themselves, Kaz. You have to practice them."

"I *know*," Kaz said. "And I will practice."

"When?" Beckett asked.

"Later," Kaz said.

Claire skipped back into her room. "Are you ready to go, Kaz?" She twisted the top off her water bottle and held it out to him.

Beckett folded his arms across his chest.

"I *have* to go to school with Claire," Kaz told Beckett. "We have a case to solve. That case could help me find my family." Not that he needed Beckett's permission. Beckett wasn't his parent. He wasn't even Kaz's grandparent.

"Fine. Go." Beckett waved his hand. "We *will* work on those skills later!"

"Sure," Kaz said. He shrank down . . . down . . . down until he was small enough to fit inside Claire's water bottle. Claire twisted the bottle closed, grabbed her bag, and thundered down the stairs.

"Bye, Grandma," she called as she reached for the door.

"Have a good day, dear," Grandma Karen said as she walked into the entryway. Claire's grandma was the librarian there. She was a lot like Kaz's grandma, except she had a pink stripe in her hair. And she wasn't a ghost.

"Is your ghost friend in there?" Grandma Karen peered into the water bottle that hung from Claire's shoulder.

Claire's grandma couldn't see Kaz, but she knew all about him. And, she

knew that Claire could see ghosts when they weren't glowing.

Grandma Karen used to see ghosts, too, when she was Claire's age, but she couldn't see them anymore. Grandma Karen also knew that Claire was trying to help Kaz find his family.

Claire's parents didn't know any of that. They were detectives, but they weren't around very often because they had big cases of their own to solve. None of their cases involved ghosts. They didn't believe in ghosts.

"We've got a case to solve at school," Claire told her grandma. "Someone saw a ghost there, so we want to see if it's someone in Kaz's family."

"How exciting," Grandma Karen said. She talked above Kaz's head. "I hope you find your family, Kaz."

Claire lifted her bottle so Kaz could see her grandma better.

"Me too," said Kaz, even though he knew Grandma Karen couldn't hear him.

* * * * * * * * * * * * * *

Claire's school was bigger than the old schoolhouse. *Noisier,* too! Kaz had to put his hands over his ears to block out all the footsteps, voices, and banging doors.

Claire stopped in front of a wall of metal doors and set Kaz's water bottle on the floor so she could take off her jacket.

"Aaaah!" Kaz yelled as a bunch of giant FEET rushed toward him. "Pick me up, Claire! PICK ME UP!" He covered his head with his hands.

"Why? What's the matter?" Claire grabbed the bottle.

The boy next to Claire gave her a funny look.

Kaz knew he had to be careful about talking to Claire in front of other solids. If she answered him, other solids would wonder who she was talking to. They would think she was weird.

But Kaz couldn't help himself. "All those feet," he said, peeking out between his fingers. "I'm afraid someone will step on me or kick me down the hall."

Claire lowered her voice. "Okay, I'll put you inside my locker." She moved Kaz's bottle to the floor of her open locker. "Better?"

"Yes. Much better," Kaz said.

Claire hung her jacket on a hook way above Kaz, then picked up the bottle again. "Okay," she said cheerfully, as she twisted the cap off. "Time to go find a ghost."

Kaz huddled at the bottom of the bottle. "I think I'll stay here," he said.

"Inside the bottle? You'll never find the ghost in there," Claire said.

Kaz didn't care. Claire's school was too noisy. Too bright. And too crowded. Kaz knew that if he came out of the bottle, all those solids would walk right through him. He *hated* it when solids walked through him.

"Remember, that ghost could be someone in your family," Claire said.

Kaz moaned. He *did* want to find his family.

"I'll take you to our cafetorium." Claire slammed the metal door closed and Kaz jumped. "It'll be quieter there. Plus, that's where Jonathan saw the ghost yesterday, so that's a good place to start looking."

"What's a cafetorium?" Kaz asked.

He'd heard her use that word before, but he didn't understand what it was.

"It's where we eat lunch, have assemblies, and do our plays," Claire said. "We've got a big stage in there and everything."

Kaz could only imagine.

Claire carried Kaz into a large room with a bunch of tables and chairs. It *was* quieter there than it had been in that hallway.

One wall of the cafetorium had stairs leading up to what looked like another room. A large red curtain covered most of that room. That was probably the stage.

There were two solids talking near the stage. One was a grown-up, the other was about Claire and Kaz's age.

"Is that Jonathan?" Kaz tilted his head toward the younger solid.

"No, I think that boy's name is Andy," Claire said in a low voice. "He's a sixth-grader. He's going to do lights and sound for our play."

Do what *with the lights and the sound?* Kaz wondered.

"The guy with the beard is Mr. Hartshorn," Claire went on. "He

teaches fifth grade. He's also our director."

Mr. Hartshorn was doing all the talking. Andy just nodded a lot.

Rrrring! Rrrring! A loud bell sounded above their heads.

"Why is that bell ringing?" Kaz asked, holding his hands to his ears. "And why is it so LOUD?"

"Because it's time for me to go to class," Claire told Kaz. "Now, do you really want to stay in that bottle all day? Or do you want to go look for ghosts?"

Kaz knew he shouldn't be such a scaredy-ghost. He'd come to school with Claire to search for his family.

Kaz swallowed hard. "I'll look for ghosts," he said bravely, as he swam out of the bottle.

"Good," Claire said. "I'll be in room 125 if you need me."

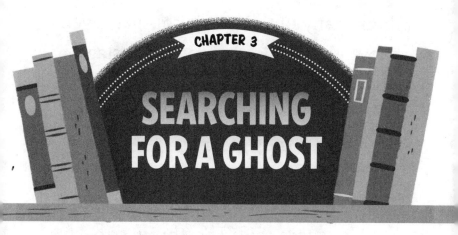

CHAPTER 3

SEARCHING FOR A GHOST

D o we get to use special effects in this play?" Andy asked Mr. Hartshorn as Kaz hovered nearby.

"Special effects?" Mr. Hartshorn scratched his chin.

"Yeah. Like smoke or trapdoors," Andy said. He shivered as Kaz drifted closer.

Mr. Hartshorn smiled. "No. We're just doing lights and sound. We don't need a trapdoor in *Jack and the Beanstalk*. I don't

think many of the kids in this play even know we have a trapdoor in the stage. And I'd like to keep it that way. For safety reasons."

"Okay," Andy groaned.

"Let me show you the control room. Quick! Before the second bell rings," Mr. Hartshorn said. They hurried to the back of the cafetorium.

Kaz swam behind them.

Mr. Hartshorn unlocked a small room and they stepped inside. Kaz hovered in the doorway. He saw a long table with a machine that had lots of buttons and knobs on it. A window above all those buttons and knobs looked out into the cafetorium. There was another door in the back wall. Probably a closet.

"Do you know how to use this equipment?" Mr. Hartshorn asked.

"Yes," Andy replied. "And I'd like to run lights and sound for the play, but I have soccer on Mondays and Wednesdays. Do you need me at every rehearsal?"

"Not until the week of the play," Mr. Hartshorn said.

Kaz backstroked away from the control room.

"Mom? Pops? Grandmom? Grandpop?" he called as he wafted around the cafetorium. "Finn? Little John? Are any of you here?"

Kaz spotted another room along the sidewall of the cafetorium. A light shined through an open doorway, and Kaz smelled something interesting. Food of some sort.

Ghosts didn't need food, but Kaz had spent enough time with Claire's family to know that solids did. In fact, solids ate food quite *often*. Sometimes more than three times a day.

Kaz swam into the room, and a loud bell rang again. But the solid ladies in this room didn't even react to the bell. They were busy stirring pans on a stove and talking about their grandchildren. Kaz watched them for a while, but then a shuffling noise outside the kitchen caught his attention. He swam back out into the cafetorium. The shuffling came from behind the heavy red curtain on the stage.

"Hello?" he said as he swam to the curtain. "Is anybody back there?"

Kaz didn't want to pass through the curtain, so he dove down and glided under it. There were even more curtains behind that first one. The whole stage was surrounded by black and gold curtains.

Kaz heard more shuffling. Then a scratching sound.

He followed the sounds to a small room behind the stage. A large board that was painted to look like a house rested against the wall outside that room. Inside, the room was piled high with boxes. Two solid girls around Kaz and Claire's age were folding clothes and putting them into boxes on the floor.

"It's not fair," grumbled the shorter girl. She had a splash of freckles on her cheeks.

"I try out for the play every year, but I never get a part. I always get stuck working backstage."

"I like working backstage," the other girl said as she tossed her long hair over her shoulder. "It's better than being on the stage and having to learn all those lines. Plus, Mr. Hartshorn lets you out of class to clean the storage room."

The girl with the freckles wrinkled her nose. "I'd rather be onstage!" she said as she shoved a box across the room.

Kaz darted out of the way.

"Besides," the girl with the freckles went on. "Mr. Hartshorn only lets us out of class because he doesn't want to clean the storage room himself!"

"Well, go back to class, then, if you don't want to help," the other girl said.

The two girls worked in silence after that.

There clearly weren't any ghosts backstage, so Kaz swam back under the curtain and into the cafetorium. He looked around. There were no ghosts in here, either.

He drifted over to the open door and *streeeetched* his head around the doorjamb and into the hallway. Kaz didn't see any ghosts. Or solids.

He wafted out into the hallway. "Mom? Pops?" Kaz called.

Some of the classroom doors were open and some were closed. Kaz swam over to a closed door and peered into the window. He saw a bunch of solid children sitting at tables and reading from books.

He checked the classroom across the hall and saw more solid children building houses out of those tiny white cubes that Claire liked to put in her hot chocolate. Kaz

couldn't remember what they were called.

Farther down the hall he heard music. A piano. And some instruments that made clomping sounds.

Kaz swam into that classroom and watched a solid boy strike a silver triangle. There was a triangle back at the old schoolhouse. Sometimes Grandpop played it for Kaz.

Thinking of Grandpop made Kaz's heart ache. It also reminded Kaz that he was here to find a ghost, not listen to music. He returned to the hallway.

He rounded a corner and came to a library. Kaz could tell it was a library because of all the books, tables, chairs, couches, and computers.

Kaz floated among groups of solid children who were working at different tables. Some had books propped open

in front of them. Some wrote in notebooks like Claire's. Some typed on computers. And some simply talked among themselves.

All of a sudden, Kaz heard a girl's voice behind him: "Hey, Ghost Boy!"

Kaz whirled around. Was that girl talking to *him*? Could she see him?

No.

She was talking to a boy with light hair who sat alone at a table, reading a book.

"Seen any more ghosts lately?" The girl poked him in the back. Her two friends giggled as they all scurried away.

The boy's face turned bright red.

Can that *boy see ghosts?* Kaz wondered. Was that Jonathan, the boy who told Claire he saw a ghost in this school yesterday?

Kaz drifted over to the boy. "Hello?" he said, gazing into the boy's eyes.

"Can you see me? Can you hear me?"

The boy turned a page in his book. He didn't act like he could see or hear Kaz.

So why did that girl call him "Ghost Boy"?

Kaz noticed a wadded-up piece of paper on the floor near the boy's feet. He saw the word *ghost* in one of the crinkles.

Is that a clue? Had the boy written something about the ghost he saw on that paper?

Kaz tried to open the paper, but his hand passed through it.

He groaned.

Kaz could almost hear Beckett's voice in his head telling him to concentrate. He *tried* to concentrate. He stared so hard at the paper that his eyes blurred. Then, biting his lip, he reached out and tried again to open the paper.

Once again, his hand passed through.

"If you have books to check out, bring them to Mrs. Coombs," one of the grown-up solids said. "It's time to go back to the room."

"Ghost Boy" grabbed the wad of paper, tossed it into a trash can on top of a bunch of other papers, then joined the crowd of kids around the big desk.

Kaz would never find out what that paper said now.

A WORD WITH "GHOST BOY"

Kaz couldn't stop thinking about that wad of paper. It could be an important clue. But he couldn't pick it up. He couldn't unfold it. And as he floated above the trash can, Kaz wasn't even sure which wad of paper was the one he wanted anymore.

What if he was letting an important clue slip away?

Maybe Claire could help. She said she would be in room 125. All Kaz had to do

was find room 125 and tell Claire about the wad of paper. Then *she* could find the right paper, open it up, and decide whether it was important.

Kaz read the numbers on the signs outside each classroom door: 108 . . . 110 . . . 112. Claire's classroom didn't appear to be down that hallway, so he tried a different one: 120 . . . 122 . . . 124 . . . and across the hall he saw 125. Kaz swam over, but there weren't any solids in room 125. Just rows of empty desks.

Where's Claire? Kaz wondered. He was sure she'd said she'd be in room 125. Was she lost? Did she leave the school without him? She wouldn't do that, would she?

Kaz didn't know what to do. He hovered outside room 125, wondering if Claire would come back.

He waited . . . and waited . . . and waited . . .

Soon he heard voices at the end of the hall. He looked up and saw a line of solid children walking toward him. Claire was second in line, right behind a grown-up solid.

"Claire!" Kaz said, swimming alongside her. "You have to come with me. I think I found a clue in the library, but I can't

open it. I can't even find it because it's in a trash can with all these other wads of paper. Come on!"

"I can't," Claire mouthed at him. "I have to stay with my class."

"What? Why?" Kaz asked.

Claire didn't answer. It was so hard to communicate with Claire when other solids were around.

Kaz followed Claire into room 125 and over to a desk in the middle of the room. As soon as she sat down, Claire stuck her hand in the air.

Kaz darted out of the way before Claire's hand passed through him.

"Mrs. Galway?" Claire said.

"Yes?" said the grown-up solid at the front of the room.

"Can I go to the bathroom?" Claire asked.

"Go quickly," Mrs. Galway said.

"Everyone else, please take out your math books."

Desks creaked open all around the room as Claire got up from her seat and hurried to the door.

Kaz swam behind her.

"Remember, I can't talk to you when other people are around," Claire whispered once they were out in the hallway.

Kaz knew that.

"And I can't go with you whenever I want to," Claire added. "I have to stay with my class unless I have permission to go someplace by myself."

"Oh," Kaz said. He *didn't* know that.

"But we're alone now," Claire said. "So, tell me about this clue."

Kaz told Claire all about the boy in the library and the wad of paper with the word *ghost* on it.

"That sounds like Jonathan," Claire said as they turned a corner. They were outside the library now. "I heard people calling him Ghost Boy in the hall this morning."

"We have to find out what he wrote on that paper. You have to come in here and find the paper he put in the trash can," Kaz said.

Claire glanced up and down the hallway. "Okay," she said. "But we have to do it quick. If Mrs. Galway finds out I went to the library instead of the bathroom, I could get in trouble."

There wasn't anyone in the library now. Kaz led Claire over to the trash can. "It's in there," he said.

Claire reached into the trash can and pulled out several wads of paper.

"That's not it," Kaz said as she unfolded the first one.

She tossed it back and opened another.

"That's not it, either," Kaz said.

Claire opened a third wad.

"That's it!" Kaz exclaimed as he saw the word *ghost*.

Claire smoothed the paper against her leg, then held it up so she could read it. She frowned. "It's a book report. Or the start of one. It's about a book called *The Ghost at Mike's House*." She dropped the paper back into the trash can.

"So it's not a clue?" Kaz asked.

"No," Claire said.

Kaz groaned. "I've been all over your school and I haven't found any ghosts or any clues."

"We need more information," Claire said. "I'll talk to Jonathan at lunch. He's the one who saw the ghost. Maybe he'll give us a clue."

* * * * * * * * * * * * * * * *

The cafetorium was a lot noisier now. A lot more crowded, too. Kaz had to swim up near the hot lights in the ceiling so no one would walk through him.

Claire stood in the middle of the room with her tray and looked around for Jonathan.

"There he is!" Kaz pointed at a boy who was sitting by himself at a table in

the far corner of the cafetorium. "That's the boy I saw in the library."

Claire nodded. "That's Jonathan." She walked over to him.

"Is it okay if I sit here?" Claire asked Jonathan as she set her tray down on his table.

Kaz floated above them.

Jonathan glanced up at Claire in surprise. "I guess," he said with a shrug. Then he turned back to his lunch.

Claire sat down. "I heard you saw a ghost during tryouts yesterday," she said as she opened her milk carton.

Jonathan looked weary. "I know you don't believe it," he said.

"No, I do!" Claire said right away. "I do believe it."

"You do?"

Claire nodded. "I've seen ghosts before,

too." She opened her bag and pulled out one of her notebooks. "Here," she said, sliding it across the table. "These are all the ghosts I've seen."

Jonathan opened the book. He studied each page.

"Tell me about the ghost you saw," Claire said as she stirred the mashed potatoes on her plate.

Kaz thought mashed potatoes were very interesting. He knew they were food. And solids ate food. But whenever Claire had mashed potatoes on her plate, she stirred them into mountains and volcanoes. And they stayed that shape until Claire ate them.

Jonathan slid the book back over to Claire. "She didn't look like any of the ghosts in there," he said.

"She?" Claire said. "So the ghost was a girl?"

"More like a lady," Jonathan said.

"What did she look like?" Claire pushed her tray away, then grabbed a pencil from her bag and turned to a blank page in her notebook.

"Like a mom," Jonathan said.

Like my *mom?* Kaz wondered.

"She was kind of bluish-white," Jonathan went on. "Or whitish-blue. Really shimmery."

"She was glowing!" Kaz exclaimed. Which meant Jonathan saw a *real* ghost.

And that ghost wanted Jonathan to see her. Ghosts never glowed unless they wanted solids to see them.

Claire drew a face in her ghost book. "What was her hair like?" she asked.

"Curly," Jonathan replied. He popped a forkful of meat into his mouth.

"Like this?" Claire drew long corkscrew curls all around her ghost's shoulders.

"No, it was shorter than that," Jonathan said, his mouth full of half-chewed food. "And the top of her hair stood straight up."

Claire drew an *X* over her drawing and turned to a new page in her notebook. "More like this?" she asked as she drew a new face with tight curls around the forehead.

"Yes."

"What was she wearing?" Claire asked.

"I don't know," Jonathan said. "Regular mom clothes. Pants and a shirt. Oh! She had a necklace with a really big heart on it."

"My mom wears a necklace with a big heart on it," Kaz said as Claire drew a necklace with a heart on the ghost.

"Bigger than that," Jonathan said.

Claire erased the heart and drew it bigger.

"Yeah, like that," Jonathan said. "She had big earrings, too. They were shaped like keys."

Kaz could hardly believe his ears. "*My mom* wears earrings that are shaped like keys!" he cried. How many other lady ghosts wear earrings like that?

Jonathan had to have seen Kaz's mom. He *had to* have.

"Ask him where he saw the ghost," Kaz said to Claire.

"Where did you see her?" Claire asked.

"Up there." Jonathan turned in his chair and pointed toward the top of the red stage curtain. "She floated through the curtain and then all around this room. And then she disappeared."

Kaz swam to the stage. "Mom?" he called as he darted under the curtain. "Mom? Are you here?" He'd already searched back there, but he had searched down low. He had *not* searched up high.

Kaz drifted slowly to the ceiling. He didn't see any ghosts, but he did see something else floating high in the air.

A bead. A whitish-blue *ghost* bead.

Just like the beads on the necklace Kaz's mom wore.

CHAPTER 5

A GHOSTLY WARNING

Kaz grabbed the bead and squeezed it in his hand.

"Mom!" he called, looking all around. "MOM!"

Kaz swam back under the curtain, through the cafetorium, and out into the hallway. "MOM! It's me, Kaz. Where are you?"

"Did you find her?" Claire asked as she joined Kaz in the hallway.

There weren't any other solids around,

so Kaz could talk freely. "No, but I found this." He opened his hand so Claire could see the ghost bead. "It's from my mom's necklace."

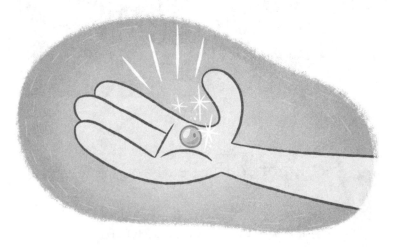

Claire's eyes grew large. "Where did you find it?"

"Up by the ceiling on the other side of that curtain."

Claire's eyes grew even larger. "That's where Jonathan saw the ghost yesterday. He must have seen your mom."

"I think so, too," Kaz said.

Claire grinned. "Well, don't just hover here in the hallway. Go find her!"

"Okay!" Kaz said. He put the bead in his pocket and swam away.

"Mom?" he called as he swam up one hallway and down another. "Mom? Are you here?"

But his mom didn't come out when Kaz called her. And Kaz couldn't find her anywhere.

He checked all the classrooms a second time. He checked the library. He checked the bathrooms. Even the bathrooms that said GIRLS on the door. He called for his mom again and again.

But he never found her. Or any other ghost.

That could mean only one thing: His mom wasn't at Claire's school anymore.

So, where did she go? Kaz wondered.

Did she accidentally blow into the Outside through an open window? Did Jonathan scare her away? Or did she go into the Outside on purpose? Maybe she was searching for Kaz and the rest of their family just like Kaz was. Maybe she went into the Outside because she wanted the wind to carry her to another building.

A loud bell rang. Classroom doors banged open and kids poured into the hallways. Kaz really hated those bells. He swam to the ceiling so no one would accidentally pass through him. He wrapped his hand around the ghost bead in his pocket.

School was done for the day.

Kaz glided along the ceiling until he found Claire. She was by her locker, putting papers into her bag.

Claire smiled at Kaz. She turned

her back to all the kids in the hall and whispered to Kaz, "Did you find your mom?"

Kaz shook his head. "I don't think she's here anymore," he said glumly.

"I'm sorry," Claire said.

* * * * * * * * * * * * * * *

Kaz held the ghost bead in his hand and gazed out the big cafetorium windows into the Outside. He'd been so close to finding his mom. *So close.*

He didn't dare go into the Outside to look for her. Who knew where the wind would carry him? It was bad enough that he'd lost his family. He didn't want to lose Claire, too.

Instead, Kaz drifted around the cafetorium and watched the kids who were working on the play. They had

divided themselves into two groups:
(1) performers and (2) backstage workers.

Claire sat with the performers. They had pushed two big tables together and were reading their parts out loud. The backstage workers sat around another table and talked about the props they would need and the sets they would build and how they would build them.

Mr. Hartshorn strolled back and forth between the two groups.

"We need a sword," said a boy in a red shirt. He was one of the backstage workers.

"A sword?" A girl with a ponytail tilted her head at him. "What for?"

"For Jack to fight the giant!" the boy replied. "Duh!"

"We also need a house for Jack and his mom," another girl said. She turned to Mr. Hartshorn. "Could we use that same house we used for *Hansel and Gretel*? I saw the pieces for it backstage."

"Sure, Kenya," Mr. Hartshorn said. "We've used that house in several different plays. I'll set it up onstage before our next rehearsal."

"We need a beanstalk, too," said a boy with glasses. "It shouldn't be hard to make one. We just need a pole. We can cut a bunch of leaves out of green construction paper and tape them to the pole. Then voilà! We have a beanstalk."

"Good idea, Ethan," said Mr. Hartshorn. "Is anyone writing all this down?"

"I can," said the girl with the ponytail. She grabbed a notebook from under her chair.

"Thanks, Gia," said Mr. Hartshorn.

"I'll make the sword!" said the boy in the red shirt. "Write that down."

Gia rolled her eyes. "Noah is making a sword," she said as she wrote.

Just then, the square box above the stage crackled. A voice inside the box called out, "Mr. Hartshorn?"

"Yes?" Mr. Hartshorn replied.

Kaz swam up to the box.

"Could you please come to the office?" the voice asked. "You've got a phone call."

Kaz tried to see inside the box. *Is someone in there?* Unfortunately, he couldn't see inside. He sure wasn't going to pass through the box to find out who or what was inside.

"I'll be right back," Mr. Hartshorn told the kids as he walked around the maze of tables. But as he reached the door, he nearly ran into a girl who was coming into the cafetorium.

"Oh, I'm sorry, Amber," Mr. Hartshorn said to the girl.

It was the girl with the freckles that Kaz had seen in the storage room earlier that morning. The one who didn't like working backstage.

"I left something in the storage room this morning," she said to Mr. Hartshorn. "Could you please unlock it?"

"I have to take a phone call right now. I'll give you my keys and you can unlock it," Mr. Hartshorn said as he felt around his pockets. He frowned. "Where *are* my keys? Did I ever get them back from you this morning?"

"Yes," Amber said.

"They're over here! You left them on our table." Noah waved a set of keys in the air.

"Go get them from Noah," Mr. Hartshorn told Amber as he left the cafetorium.

Noah tossed the keys to Amber, and she headed for the stage. The performers returned to their scripts, and the backstage workers returned to their discussion about props.

All of a sudden there was a scream backstage.

Everyone turned.

"Amber?" Gia called as she hopped to her feet. "Are you okay?"

The kids raced across the cafetorium, up to the stage, and back behind the curtain. Kaz swam just above their heads.

"Is that someone's idea of a joke?" Amber pointed at the back wall of the storage room.

A pair of creepy-looking eyes had been drawn onto the back wall in some strange, bright, whitish-blue substance. Below the eyes were the words: BEWARE. I'M HERE. AND I'M WATCHING. Many of the letters appeared to drip down the wall.

"Who's here?" Claire asked. "Who's watching?"

"A ghoooooost!" Noah said.

Amber elbowed him. "Did you do this?" she asked.

"Me?" Noah laughed. "When would I have?"

"Just now," Amber said. "Mr. Hartshorn's keys were lying on the table. Right by you."

"I've been here talking about props this whole time," Noah said. "What about you, Amber? You're the one who was late. Mr. Hartshorn's keys were sitting right there. Anyone could've put them there,

including you! Plus, you can get paint at your dad's paint store. You probably don't even have to pay for it."

"I gave Mr. Hartshorn his keys back this morning," Amber said. "I was late because I had safety patrol. Ask anyone. I was outside until, like, five minutes ago. And just because my dad owns a paint store doesn't prove anything. Are you sure that's even paint on the wall?"

Ethan touched the *B* in the word *Beware*. "Whatever it is, it's still wet." He held out his smudged finger for everyone to see. "It feels like slime. Glow-in-the-dark slime."

"Hey, let's see if it really does glow in the dark," Noah said. He flipped the light switch and the room went dark.

"Aaaaahhhh!" several kids shrieked as the dripping words and creepy eyes glowed bright.

"Turn the light on! Turn the light on!" someone cried.

Claire flipped the switch and the light came back on.

"You know what I think it is?" Noah asked.

"What?" several kids asked at the same time.

"GHOST BLOOD!" Noah cried as he lunged at Jonathan. "I think Ghost Boy's ghost wrote that message in ghost blood!"

Jonathan shrank back.

"Ewww!" squealed one of the girls.

"It does kind of look like ghost blood," Gia said in a small voice.

Claire studied the message on the wall.

"There's no such thing as ghost blood," Kaz told her. But he had to admit the creepy eyes and the drippy words were the same color as ghosts when they glowed.

"Has your ghost been back, Ghost Boy?" Ethan asked Jonathan.

"Wooooooooooo!" Several kids raised their hands and pretended to be ghosts. Others laughed.

Jonathan's face grew red.

"What's going on?" Mr. Hartshorn came up behind them. "Why are you all backstage?" His jaw tightened as he read the ghostly message. "Who wrote that?" he asked, glancing at each student.

Silence.

Mr. Hartshorn frowned. "Well, if no one is going to admit responsibility, I think you can all go get some cleaning supplies from the janitor's closet and clean it up."

"All of us?" Ethan said. "We *all* have to clean it up even though we didn't do it?"

"Yes," Mr. Hartshorn said. "Rehearsal is over for today."

CHAPTER 6

THE GHOST COMES BACK

o, did you bring home any more lost ghosts?" Beckett asked as he met Kaz and Claire in the library entryway. Claire twisted the top off the bottle, and Kaz swam out and expanded to his normal size.

Kaz's ghost dog and Claire's solid cat scampered over to greet them.

Claire gave Thor's ears a quick scratch.

"No," Kaz said glumly. He rubbed Cosmo's belly.

"We need to talk about this case," Claire said as she headed for the craft room. Kaz, Beckett, and Cosmo followed.

Claire sat down at the table. "I don't know about you, Kaz, but I think Jonathan saw a real ghost."

Kaz agreed.

"And I think the ghost he saw was probably your mom," Claire said.

Kaz agreed with that, too.

"But you searched the whole school and you didn't find her," Claire went on.

"That's because she's not there anymore," Kaz said.

"Well, that's what I thought . . . until we saw that message after school," Claire said.

"My mom didn't write that message," Kaz said. His mom would never draw creepy eyes on a wall or write a scary message.

"What message?" Beckett asked.

"Someone wrote, 'Beware. I'm here. And I'm watching' on a wall at my school," Claire said. "We don't know who wrote it. It could've been a ghost."

"It wasn't a ghost," Kaz said.

Claire unzipped her bag and pulled out her clues notebook. "Let's write down everything we know about this case,"

she said. "The things we know *for sure.*
Maybe that'll give us a clue about who
could have written it."

Kaz and Beckett hovered above Claire
as she wrote:

1. *Jonathan saw a ghost in the cafetorium
   yesterday.*
2. *Kaz found a bead that belongs to his mom.
   He found it close to where Jonathan saw the
   ghost yesterday.*

"You found a bead that belongs to
your mother?" Beckett asked.

"Yes." Kaz reached into his pocket and
pulled out the ghost bead.

"How do you know it's your
mother's?" Beckett reached for the bead,
but Kaz held tight to it.

"I just do," Kaz said, slipping the bead
back inside his pocket. He knew his
mom's necklace when he saw it.

Claire kept writing:

3. *Someone drew two eyes and wrote "Beware. I'm here. And I'm watching" in—*

Claire raised her head. "We don't know what they wrote it with. Maybe paint. But maybe ghost blood."

"Ghost blood!" Beckett sniffed. "There's no such thing as ghost blood."

"That's what I told her," Kaz said. "But it did kind of glow. You know, like ghosts do."

Claire added:

—something. We don't know what they wrote it in.

Then she moved on to number four. "We're pretty sure the storage room was locked," she said out loud as she wrote.

"But Mr. Hartshorn's keys were on the table," Kaz said. "A girl named Amber

thought that a boy named Noah took them and wrote the message. And Noah thought Amber did it."

Claire set down her pencil and leaned back against her chair. "Anyone could have taken Mr. Hartshorn's keys and written that message. Or . . . a ghost could've passed through the wall or the door and written it."

Kaz didn't think a ghost had done it, but he didn't want to argue with Claire.

"You should come to school with me again tomorrow and look for more clues," Claire told Kaz.

"No," Beckett said, shaking his head. "Absolutely not. Kaz already had a day off from his ghost skills. He can't take another day off."

"You know what, Beckett?" Claire said, her hands on her hips. "You're not the

boss of Kaz. If he wants to come to school with me, he can!"

"That's right," Kaz said. He decided he *would* go to school with Claire again tomorrow. He would try to figure out who wrote that message on the storage-room wall. Maybe he'd even find more beads from his mom's necklace.

* * * * * * * * * * * * * * * * *

The next day, while Claire was in class, Kaz searched her school for clues. And for beads.

He didn't find any clues or beads.

After school, he watched Claire's rehearsal again. Today, the red curtain was open and there was a small house in the middle of the stage. *Jack's house.* Kaz floated all around it. He was surprised to see the back was completely open.

The performers walked around on the stage and read from their scripts. Mr. Hartshorn stopped them often and told them where to stand and what to do.

"Scene four," Mr. Hartshorn called. "Jonathan, I want you to enter stage right. Claire, you enter stage left."

Kaz watched as Jonathan and Claire walked onto the stage from opposite directions.

"Let's start with your line, Claire," Mr. Hartshorn said.

"Jack—" Claire began. Her forehead wrinkled and she glanced over her shoulder. "What's that noise?"

"That's not your line." A girl with red hair squinted at the script in her hand.

"I know," Claire said. "I'm asking for real. What's that noise? Don't you hear it? It sounds like music."

Everyone stopped talking and listened. It did sound like music. Piano music. It came from somewhere backstage.

Claire went behind the stage and followed the sound of the music. Everyone else, including Mr. Hartshorn and Kaz, followed her.

Claire stopped suddenly. There, in the far back corner, stood a tall piano. The keys on the piano were moving. All by themselves.

"No one is playing that piano," Ethan said.

"Uh-huh," Jonathan said, wide-eyed. "A GHOST is playing it!"

Kaz didn't see any ghosts.

"Wooooooooooooo!" said Noah, pretending to be a ghost. "Beware! I'm heeere and I'm waaaatching."

Claire scowled at Noah, then moved

closer to Jonathan. "Do you really see a ghost over there, Jonathan?" she asked.

"No," Jonathan admitted. "But I saw one in here the other day."

Several kids snickered.

"I did," Jonathan insisted. He moved to the back of the crowd.

"There's no ghost," Mr. Hartshorn said as he strode over to the piano. "This is a player piano. It plays music by itself." He felt around on the side of the piano, and the music stopped. "See? I just turned it off. Now I'd like to know who turned it on."

The kids all looked at one another. Nobody said a word.

"No one?" Mr. Hartshorn asked.

"I didn't even know it was a player piano," Amber mumbled.

"Neither did I," Noah said.

"Maybe we really do have a ghost

in our school," Ethan said with a shrug.

"There's no such thing as ghosts," Mr. Hartshorn said.

Kaz hated it when solids said that. It was like saying there's no such thing as solids.

The kids slowly drifted back to their places on the stage. But before they could pick up where they'd left off, a bright light shined onto the stage from the little room at the back of the cafetorium.

Some kids squinted. Others put their hands up to block the light.

"Who turned on that spotlight?" Mr. Hartshorn asked as he jumped down from the stage and marched to the back of the cafetorium. "Is someone messing around in the control room?"

Mr. Hartshorn reached for the doorknob, but the door was locked.

CHAPTER 7

A SURPRISING NEW SKILL

Mr. Hartshorn unlocked the control-room door and stepped inside. Kaz peeked in behind him. He didn't see anyone, ghost or solid, in there.

Mr. Hartshorn switched off the spotlight, then peered under the counter and behind the door. He even opened the closet at the back of the control room. He stood there for a long time, which seemed strange because the closet was obviously empty.

"There's no one in the control room,"
Mr. Hartshorn said when he returned to
the cafetorium. "The door was locked.
And this time I had my keys with me. So
how did that spotlight come on? I know
it didn't turn on by itself."

Nobody offered any ideas.

Mr. Hartshorn sighed. "Fine. Let's get back to work. I don't want any more funny business!"

Claire and Jonathan returned to their places onstage. Other kids sat down on the floor in front of the stage and on the steps. And the kids who were working on props went back to painting leaves and cutting them out.

Noah grabbed the sword he'd cut out of cardboard and swung it around. "If there's a ghost at our school, I'll find it and stab it with my magic sword!"

Kaz shivered.

"No stabbing," Mr. Hartshorn said. "And no more talk about ghosts."

"Aww," Noah whined.

Kaz didn't like Noah very much. He didn't like the way Noah teased Jonathan, but he *really* didn't like what Noah said

about finding "the ghost" and stabbing it. Kaz knew Noah couldn't see him, but he decided to stay as far away from Noah as he could.

* * * * * * * * * * * * * * * *

That night, Claire did her homework in the craft room while Kaz practiced his ghost skills with Beckett.

"Can a ghost turn on a player piano or a spotlight?" Claire asked the ghosts.

"Of course," Beckett replied. "It's just a matter of moving a solid object. Show her, Kaz. Go over there and turn off that table lamp."

"I can't!" Kaz moaned. And Beckett knew he couldn't.

"Try," Beckett insisted.

Kaz floated over the table. He stared hard at the lamp.

"Come on, Kaz," Claire cheered him on. "You can do it."

Kaz held his breath, clenched his teeth, and sent all his energy to his finger as he reached for the switch. His finger passed through the base of the lamp. "See?" he said.

"Again," Beckett ordered. "Try it again."

Kaz sighed. He squeezed the ghost bead inside his pocket for luck, then reached for the switch again.

And once again, his finger passed through the lamp.

"Concentrate!" Beckett said.

"I am!" Kaz cried. He was concentrating so hard that the lamp blurred in front of him. He touched his finger to the switch one more time, but this time something amazing happened.

The lamp disappeared from the solid world.

Kaz, Claire, and Beckett all stared. They could still see the lamp even though it was no longer solid. In fact, they could see right through it as it floated in midair. But it wasn't brown anymore. Now it was the same whitish-blue color as Kaz, Beckett, and the bead inside Kaz's pocket.

"How did you do that?" Claire and Beckett asked at the same time.

"I-I don't know," Kaz stammered.

"No, really," Beckett said very seriously as he floated around the ghost lamp. "HOW DID YOU DO THAT?"

"I don't know," Kaz said again.

"Can you turn it back?" Claire asked.

"Can you do it again?" Beckett asked.

"I don't know!" Kaz threw up his hands. "I don't know how I did it. I don't

know if I can put it back. And I don't know if I can do it again."

"Well, first, why don't you try to make it solid again?" Beckett suggested.

"How?" Kaz asked.

"I'm not sure," Beckett said. "This isn't a skill I've ever seen before."

"Really?" Kaz gaped at Beckett. "You mean, *you* can't do it?" He grinned. "I have a skill that you don't have?"

"Well," Beckett sniffed. "I wouldn't call it a skill if you can't do it at will. Now can you return that lamp to the solid world or not?"

Since Kaz didn't know how he had made the lamp disappear from the solid world, he didn't know if he could return it. He put his hand on the lamp, concentrated really hard, and willed it to turn solid again.

Nothing happened.

"Can you make something else disappear?" Beckett asked. "Like maybe this table?"

"No!" Claire said, throwing her body over it. "People will notice if a big table is missing. They may even notice the lamp is missing. If you're going to make stuff disappear, it's got to be stuff that no one will miss. Like maybe this pencil." She held it up.

Kaz stared hard at the pencil and *sloooowly* reached for it. *Concentrate . . . concentrate . . . concentrate*, he said inside his head.

But the pencil remained solid, and Kaz's hand passed through it.

"Claire?" Grandma Karen poked her head into the craft room. "Is your homework done?"

Kaz held his breath, waiting to see if Grandma Karen would notice the missing lamp. But if she noticed, she didn't say anything.

"Yes, my homework is done," Claire said.

"Good." Grandma Karen smiled.

"Then say good night to your ghost friend because it's time for bed."

"Good night, Kaz," Claire said. Then she followed her grandma up the stairs.

All night long, Beckett pestered Kaz. "Can you make this book disappear? How about this picture on the wall? Try putting both hands on it. Okay, maybe just one hand. Are you really concentrating?"

"YES!" Kaz cried. "But I'm tired of concentrating. If you want to figure out this skill so bad, maybe *you* should work on it yourself!"

Kaz had other things to think about. Like, where did his mom go? Who wrote that message in the storage room? What did they use to write it? And who turned on the piano and the spotlight in the cafetorium?

CHAPTER 8

MORE TROUBLE BACKSTAGE

The next morning, Beckett was *still* trying to figure out how to make something disappear from the solid world.

"How close were you to that lamp when you made it disappear?" Beckett asked Kaz. "Were you hovering above it or were you beside it? Were you upside down or right side up?"

"I don't know!"

"How do you not know?" Beckett cried, pulling at his hair.

"You were there, too," Kaz pointed out. "If you don't remember, how do you expect me to?"

"Because you're the one who did it!"

"Good morning," Claire said cheerfully as she joined Kaz and Beckett in the craft room.

"Good morning," Kaz said.

Beckett grunted.

Kaz swam over to Claire. "Can I come to school with you today?" he whispered as he hovered near Claire's ear. He needed a break from Beckett.

"Of course," Claire said. "You *should* come to school. We still haven't solved the case of the backstage ghost. We can't stop until we solve the case!"

So Kaz went to school with Claire. While Claire was busy in her classroom,

Kaz drifted up and down hallways . . . in and out of classrooms . . .

He didn't find any clues. But he did find a wadded-up piece of paper on the floor in an empty hallway. He swam over and tried to pick it up. His hand passed through it.

He tried to make that paper disappear from the solid world. He stared hard at it and reached for it again.

His hand passed through it again.

What did I do differently last night to make that lamp disappear from the table in the craft room?

While he was thinking about that, he heard a familiar voice coming from the classroom behind him: "I don't know where my science book is."

Kaz glided over to the doorway to see who had said that.

It was Andy, the boy who would be working in the control room during the play.

"You haven't had your science book all week," the teacher told Andy. She did not look happy.

"I know," Andy said, his shoe digging into the floor. "I wish I knew what happened to it."

* * * * * * * * * * * * * * * *

At lunch, Kaz hovered around Claire and Jonathan. While they were talking, Noah snuck up behind Jonathan and yelled, "BOO!"

Both Claire and Jonathan jumped.

"Got you, Ghost Boy!" Noah laughed. "You jumped a mile!"

"Stop calling me 'Ghost Boy,'" Jonathan said.

96

"Ghost Boy! Ghost Boy!" Noah taunted as he walked away.

"That isn't very nice!" Claire called to Noah.

"No one's ever nice to me," Jonathan said. "Except for you. When I was in third grade, they called me Puke Boy. Because I threw up in school once. Ghost Boy is actually better."

"No, it's not," Claire said. "People shouldn't call names at all."

Kaz agreed. He wished he could make kids stop calling Jonathan "Ghost Boy." But what could he do? He was just a ghost.

Then he got an idea. He wasn't sure it would work, but it was worth a try.

Kaz floated over to Noah and . . . blew into his hair.

Surprisingly enough, the hair around Noah's ear moved a little.

Kaz blew into Noah's hair again. This time Noah reached up and pushed the piece of hair back into place.

Kaz did it again. Harder this time.

Noah shivered, then turned all around like he was trying to figure out what was making his hair move.

Claire grinned at Kaz as Noah left the cafetorium.

Kaz felt pleased with himself. He may not have figured out how to pick up a solid object or make it disappear, but he'd found a way to *move* a solid object.

* * * * * * * * * * * * * * * * *

"I'd like you all to try on costumes today," Mr. Hartshorn said at the beginning of rehearsal that afternoon. "Amber and Kenya went through all the costumes the other day. I pinned your names to the ones I'd like each of you to try on. You'll find them hanging on a rack in the storage room."

Claire and the other performers went back behind the curtain.

Kaz waited in the cafetorium. He watched the backstage workers piece together the beanstalk. They were building it right beside Jack's house.

A few minutes later, the performers wandered back onto the stage. None of them were in costume.

Mr. Hartshorn glanced up at them in surprise. "What's the matter?" he asked.

"Our costumes are missing," Claire said.

Mr. Hartshorn stood up. "What do you mean your costumes are missing? They can't *all* be missing."

"They are," said Jonathan, scratching his ear.

Several other kids nodded in agreement.

"Amber?" Mr. Hartshorn called. "Where are the costumes? Weren't they hanging in the storage room?"

Amber poked her head around the curtain. "They were," she said. "But they're not there now."

Mr. Hartshorn sighed. "Does anyone know what happened to the costumes?"

"Wooooooooooooo," Noah wailed as

he raised his hands over Jonathan and pretended to grab him.

"Stop horsing around!" Mr. Hartshorn said, and Noah quickly dropped his hands. "I don't know who's causing all this mischief, but it stops *now*. If those costumes don't show up by the end of the week, I'm going to cancel this play."

A couple of the kids gasped.

"We can't perform without costumes," Mr. Hartshorn said. "Rehearsal is over for today."

"I don't want Mr. Hartshorn to cancel the play," Claire told Kaz after everyone had left.

Kaz didn't want Mr. Hartshorn to cancel the play, either.

"We have to figure out what's going on around here," Claire said. "Let's see if we can find any clues."

Kaz had been looking for clues all week. *There* aren't *any clues in this school,* he thought. But he didn't know what else to do, so he followed Claire around the cafetorium.

They peered inside the locked control room.

Nothing appeared out of place.

They went onto the stage and back behind the curtain. "The storage-room door is probably locked, too," Claire said, checking the door.

It was.

"It's hard to look for clues when everywhere we want to search is locked," Kaz said. He followed Claire back onto the stage. As he sailed past the beanstalk, he noticed a narrow gap in the floor behind Jack's house.

Kaz swam back and took a closer look.

"Hey, Claire," he called, windmilling his arms. "Come look at this."

Claire walked over. "What's that?" she asked, dropping to her knees. She slipped her fingers inside the gap and pulled. A board in the floor started to move.

Claire pulled harder at the board. She slid it over as far as it would go . . . and revealed a hidden stairway under the stage.

"Wow," Claire said.

"I wonder what's down there," Kaz said, peering into the dark passageway.

"Let's find out." Claire reached into her bag and pulled out her phone. She shined the light from her phone onto the stairway. "This should give us enough light to see by," she said as she stepped into the opening.

"Are you sure we should go down there?" Kaz asked. "What if we get trapped?"

"Relax. We're not going to get trapped," Claire said.

Kaz wasn't good at relaxing.

"Come on." Claire waved her hand. "I want to close this door back up so no one else finds it."

Against his better judgment, Kaz

swam down into the opening, and Claire pulled the door closed over their heads.

They were in a dark, narrow tunnel. Claire shined the light from her phone all around them, stopping on a metal can a few feet away from the stairs.

"What's that?" Kaz asked, drifting closer.

Claire bent down in front of the can and read the label. "It's glow-in-the dark paint."

"That looks like the same stuff we found on the wall of the storage room," Kaz said.

"Looks like it came from Pete's Paint Shop," Claire said. She stood up. "Let's see what else is down here." She held the phone in front of her and walked deeper into the tunnel.

A couple of minutes later, they came to a large cardboard box. Claire shined her phone on a pile of folded clothes inside the box. "Hey, I think these are our missing costumes," she said as she rifled through the box with her free hand. "This one has Jonathan's name on it. This one has Sophia's name. And this one has *my* name on it. We'll come back and get the costumes once we see where this tunnel leads."

They followed the tunnel around a corner. It ended at another set of stairs. Claire put her hand on the railing and climbed the stairs. At the top was another closed door.

"This door is probably locked, too," she said, reaching for the knob.

But much to their surprise, the knob turned easily.

CHAPTER 9

CAUGHT IN THE ACT!

Claire pushed the door all the way open and stepped into another room. Kaz floated in behind her. The room looked familiar.

"We're in the control room," Claire said, turning all the way around.

Kaz glanced back at the door they'd just come through. "I thought that was a closet," he said.

"It *is* a closet," Claire said. "A closet that has a secret passageway in the

back of it. I think this explains how our 'ghost'"—Claire made quote marks in the air—"got in here to turn on the spotlight when the door was locked."

"So you don't think the ghost is really a ghost anymore?" Kaz asked.

"No." Claire shook her head.

Finally, Kaz thought.

"The question is, who *is* our ghost?" Claire asked.

"Amber?" Kaz suggested. "She was

wearing a Pete's Paint Shop shirt the other day. Noah said she could get paint at her dad's store. I bet her dad's store is Pete's Paint Shop. Plus, she was disappointed she didn't get a part in the play. I heard her tell another girl that she never gets a part, and she doesn't think it's fair that she always has to work backstage."

"Hmm. That sounds like motive," Claire said as she wandered around the tiny control room. "And—oh!" She nearly tripped over something. "What was that?" She looked down at the floor.

"A book," Kaz said. He swam down and stared hard at the cover. *Science in Our World.*

"It should say inside whose book it is," Claire said.

Kaz reached for the cover. *Concentrate,* he told himself. *Concentrate and open*

the book. But his hand passed through it.

"I'll get it." Claire picked up the book. "I bet it's Amber's book." She opened the cover and her eyebrows shot up.

"Is it Amber's?" Kaz asked.

"No." Claire shook her head. "It's Andy Jensen's book."

Kaz was confused. "Does that mean Andy is our 'ghost' instead of Amber?" He remembered that Andy was missing his science book.

"I don't know," Claire said.

Kaz couldn't think of a reason why Andy would write that message on the wall or turn on the piano or the spotlight. And he couldn't figure out *when* Andy would have done those things. Andy hadn't been to any of the rehearsals.

"Maybe Amber took Andy's science book and put it in here to make it look like he's

the ghost instead of her?" Claire suggested.

"Or maybe the science book isn't part of this case at all," Kaz said. "Maybe Andy simply left it in the control room that day he was talking to Mr. Hartshorn?"

"Maybe," Claire said. She put Andy's book in her bag. "I'll talk to both Andy and Amber tomorrow and see what we can find out."

"Sounds like a plan," Kaz said.

Claire opened the door, and she and Kaz went out into the cafetorium. The door to the control room locked behind them.

They were close to solving this case. Kaz could feel it.

* * * * * * * * * * * * * * * *

The next morning, Claire waited for Andy before school. Kaz floated safely in the water bottle at her side.

"Hey, Andy," Claire called to him, holding the science book out to him. "Is this yours?"

Andy's face brightened. "Yes!" he said, grabbing the book. "Where did you find it? I've been looking all over for it."

"It was in the control room," Claire said.

"Huh. I must've left it in there when Mr. Hartshorn showed me around."

Andy turned to leave, but Claire called him back. "Do you know anything about a secret passageway that goes between the stage and the control room in the cafetorium?" she asked.

Andy looked around nervously, then leaned close to Claire and whispered, "Do *you* know anything about a secret passageway that goes between the stage and the control room in the cafetorium?"

"Maybe," Claire said, staring hard at him.

Andy stared back. Finally, he broke the silence between them. "If you do know something about it, one, you didn't hear it from me, and two, I would recommend you *not* tell Mr. Hartshorn you know about it."

Then he walked away.

* * * * * * * * * * * * * * *

Claire couldn't talk to Amber that day because Amber was home sick.

"I guess there won't be any ghostly happenings during rehearsal today," Kaz said.

"Not if Amber is our ghost," Claire agreed.

After school, Mr. Hartshorn motioned for all the performers and backstage workers to sit down at the tables in the cafetorium. Kaz hovered above them.

"I see the costumes haven't been returned yet," Mr. Hartshorn said with disappointment.

Oh no! Kaz thought. He swam down and whispered to Claire, "We were going to go back into that tunnel and get the costumes before we left yesterday!"

Claire nodded slightly.

Kaz could tell she was disappointed they'd forgotten, too.

Claire raised her hand. "I have a feeling the costumes will be back tomorrow. Monday, at the latest."

Depending on how long Amber is sick, Kaz thought.

"Not if a ghost took them," Noah pointed out. "If a ghost took them, we'll probably never see them again."

"That's enough talk about ghosts," Mr. Hartshorn said. "Claire, I hope you're right. I hope the costumes are returned because I would hate to cancel this play. Let's rehearse."

The performers silently took their places onstage. The first half of rehearsal passed without any problems.

Then all of a sudden, the spotlight shined from the control room . . . and a

loud, ghostly *Wooooooooooooooo!* sounded throughout the cafetorium.

Mr. Hartshorn threw his script in the air in frustration. All the kids ran from the stage and the tables in the cafetorium to the control room. All the kids except for Claire.

"I guess Amber isn't the ghost after all," Kaz said to Claire. "So who is?"

"I'm going to find out," Claire said as she walked over to Jack's house.

Kaz followed.

The crack in the floor behind the house was open a couple of inches. *Someone was in the secret tunnel!*

"Hey, what are you doing, Claire?" Noah called out to her as Mr. Hartshorn unlocked the control room.

The main light came on inside the control room. The spotlight went off.

117

And the loud, ghostly *Woooooooooooooo!* stopped.

Claire didn't answer. And she didn't take her eyes off the crack in the floor.

"Yeah, what are you looking at, Claire?" Ethan asked.

A bunch of kids ran for the stage and gathered around Claire, just as the door in the stage floor started to slide open.

CHAPTER 10

ALL'S WELL THAT ENDS WELL

What the—?" Ethan said as Jonathan's head popped up through the opening in the floor.

"What are you doing, Jonathan?" Noah cried. "Are you the ghost?"

Jonathan froze.

"I thought Amber was the ghost," Claire said. "But *you're* the one who's been going back and forth between the stage and the control room, Jonathan? You're the one who turned on the spotlight and

the sound just now? And the piano the other day?"

Jonathan lowered his eyes. "Yeah," he admitted. He climbed the rest of the way out of the tunnel and sat on the floor.

"Did you write that message on the wall in the storage room, too?" Gia asked.

"Mr. Hartshorn's keys were lying on the table," Jonathan said. "I took them when no one was looking and then put them back."

"And did you hide the costumes?" Noah asked.

Jonathan nodded. He pointed down into the tunnel. "They're down there."

"How did you even know about that tunnel, Jonathan?" Mr. Hartshorn asked as he made his way through the crowd. "We haven't used it in years. I didn't think anyone in this group even knew about it."

"My brother told me about it," Jonathan replied.

Mr. Hartshorn bent down beside Jonathan. "Why, Jonathan?" he asked, putting a hand on the boy's shoulder. "You've got one of the lead roles in the play. Why would you do all this?"

"Because I really did see a ghost the day of tryouts, but no one believed me. And now everyone keeps teasing me about it." Jonathan raised his eyes. "I didn't mean any harm. I just wanted people to stop teasing me. You won't really cancel the play, will you, Mr. Hartshorn?"

Mr. Hartshorn didn't answer right away.

"I understand if you don't want me to play Jack anymore. But please don't cancel the play," Jonathan said.

Mr. Hartshorn rubbed his chin. "I won't cancel the play," he said.

"Hooray!" everyone cheered.

"And you can still play Jack . . . *if* you promise no more backstage trouble and you apologize to your castmates," Mr. Hartshorn said.

"I promise. And I'm sorry, everyone," Jonathan said.

"Good. I'm reasonably confident everyone will stop teasing you, too," Mr. Hartshorn said with a pointed look at Noah.

"Sure," Noah said, elbowing Ethan.

* * * * * * * * * * * * * * *

A couple of weeks later, Kaz went to school with Claire, her mom and dad, and Grandma Karen. They went at *night*. Inside the car.

Kaz liked riding in the car. It was like being inside a second water bottle. Kaz felt extra protected from the Outside.

When they pulled up to the school, Claire's mom said, "Break a leg, honey!" Which seemed strange to Kaz. Why would Claire's own mother want her to break a leg?

"I will!" Claire grabbed the water bottle and ran toward the school. She let Kaz out of the water bottle once they were safely inside the cafetorium. Then she went to change into her costume.

A lot of the kids had already put on

their costumes. The backstage workers bustled around, making sure all the props were in order.

"Hey, Ghost Boy!" Noah cried as he jabbed Jonathan with his cardboard sword.

"You're not supposed to be messing around with the props," Jonathan said. "And you're not supposed to tease me anymore."

Noah grinned. "Are you going to stop me, Ghost Boy?" He jabbed at Jonathan again. "Huh? Are you?"

Jonathan tried to grab the sword from Noah, but Noah backed away before Jonathan could reach it.

Kaz wished he could put Noah in his place once and for all. He swam over, reached for the sword, and . . . grabbed it right out of Noah's hand.

Noah and Jonathan both stared at the sword that appeared to be floating in midair.

But no one was more shocked than Kaz.

"I'm doing it!" Kaz laughed out loud. "I'm holding a solid object!" If only Beckett could see him now.

But as soon as he thought that, the sword fell through Kaz's hand and landed on the floor.

"Did you see that?" Noah asked as several other kids gathered around.

"Yeah, Butterfingers," Ethan said with a laugh. "Looks like you can't hold onto a sword."

Noah didn't think that was funny. "It felt like someone or *something* grabbed the sword right out of my hand."

"Like what?" Jonathan asked. "A *ghost*? Now who's the Ghost Boy?"

Claire walked over then. "Did I miss something?" she asked the boys as she tied the costume's apron around her waist.

"You guys saw it," Noah cried. "That sword was floating in midair!"

"Sure, Noah. Sure, it was," Jonathan said as he and Ethan walked away.

Noah picked up the sword and set it on the table with the other props. "It was!" he insisted as he ran after Jonathan and Ethan.

Kaz and Claire were alone.

"This is what you missed," Kaz said. He floated over to the table and picked up the cardboard sword.

Claire drew in her breath. "Wow! Good for you, Kaz. I knew you'd learn to pick up a solid object. I knew it!"

"Thanks," Kaz said as the sword fell to the table.

Now if only he could master a few more ghost skills. And find his family. He would, one day. He was sure of it.

Until then, he'd keep practicing his skills and hanging out with Claire. Who knew what kind of case would come their way next?